MR. TICK__

in a tangle

Original concept by Roger Hargreaves
Illustrated and written by Adam Hargreaves

MR. MEN   LITTLE MISS

MR. MEN™ LITTLE MISS™ © THOIP (a SANRIO company)

Mr. Tickle in a tangle © 1998 THOIP (a Sanrio company)
Printed and published under licence from Price Stern Sloan, Inc., Los Angeles.
This edition published in 2017 by Dean, an imprint of Egmont UK Limited,
The Yellow Building, 1 Nicholas Road, London W11 4AN

ISBN 978 0 6035 7408 5
67473/1
Printed in Estonia

Now, who does that extraordinarily long arm belong to?

Of course! Mr Tickle.

And Mr Tickle's long, long arms come in very handy.

They can reach kites caught in trees.

They can answer the phone when
Mr Tickle is in the bath.

But, most importantly, they are splendidly perfect for tickling!

Tickling people around corners.

Tickling people through upstairs windows.

And even tickling people on the other side of letter boxes!

However, there are days when those extraordinarily long arms are not so handy.

Days when they are nothing but a nuisance.

Days like last Monday.

Mr Tickle was lying in bed eating breakfast when he heard his garden gate open.

It was Mr Stamp, the postman.

Quick as a flash Mr Tickle sent one of his long arms down the stairs to tickle Mr Stamp.

Or, that is what he intended to do, but somehow or other, his arm got tangled up in the banisters.

Poor Mr Tickle!

It took him an hour to untangle his arm!

The letter Mr Stamp had delivered was an invitation from Mr Uppity, for lunch at the Grand Hotel.

Mr Tickle took the bus to town and sat on the upper deck.

Mr Tickle sent one of his long arms down the stairs to tickle the bus driver, but, somehow or other, the ticket inspector trod on his arm!

OUCH!

Mr Tickle arrived at the Grand Hotel and rushed through the revolving door.

Or rather he tried to, but, somehow or other, his arms caught in the door.

The fire brigade had to be called out to untangle his arms, by which time he had missed lunch.

Poor Mr Tickle.

No lunch, and even worse,

No tickles!

It was a very sad Mr Tickle who set off
for home.

Suddenly he heard something.

He stopped. Somebody was approaching
from around the corner.

Mr Tickle smiled to himself.

And sent both his arms around the corner to
tickle that somebody.

But that somebody was Little Miss Naughty.

And she tied those extraordinarily long arms together in a knot!

When he got home, Mr Tickle fell back into his armchair.

What a terrible day.

Not one tickle!

Suddenly there was a knock at the door.

It was Little Miss Tiny.

Mr Tickle stretched out one of his extraordinarily long arms.

Well, one tickle was better than none.

Even if it was only a tiny tickle!